The Shmoogly Boo

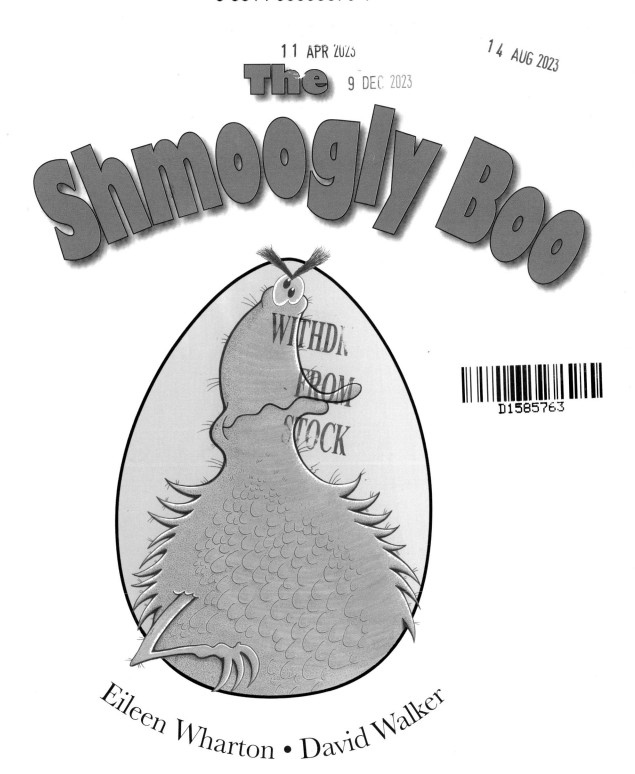

Eileen Wharton • David Walker

One day, Harry was walking in the woods when he heard an enormous:

"BOO!"

He looked to his left; he looked to his right. He looked up, and he looked down. But he couldn't work out where the noise was coming from. "Who's there?" he shouted.

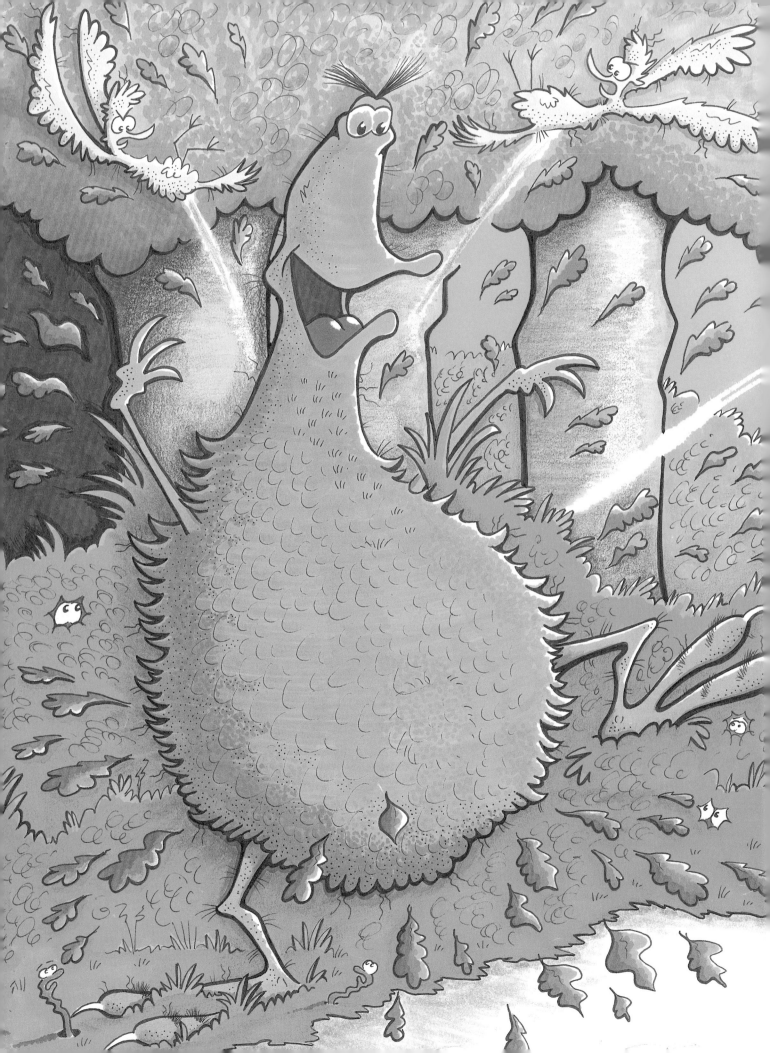

Out of the shadows stepped a huge monster, with pink eyes, no teeth, hairy toes and a fluffy, orange coat.

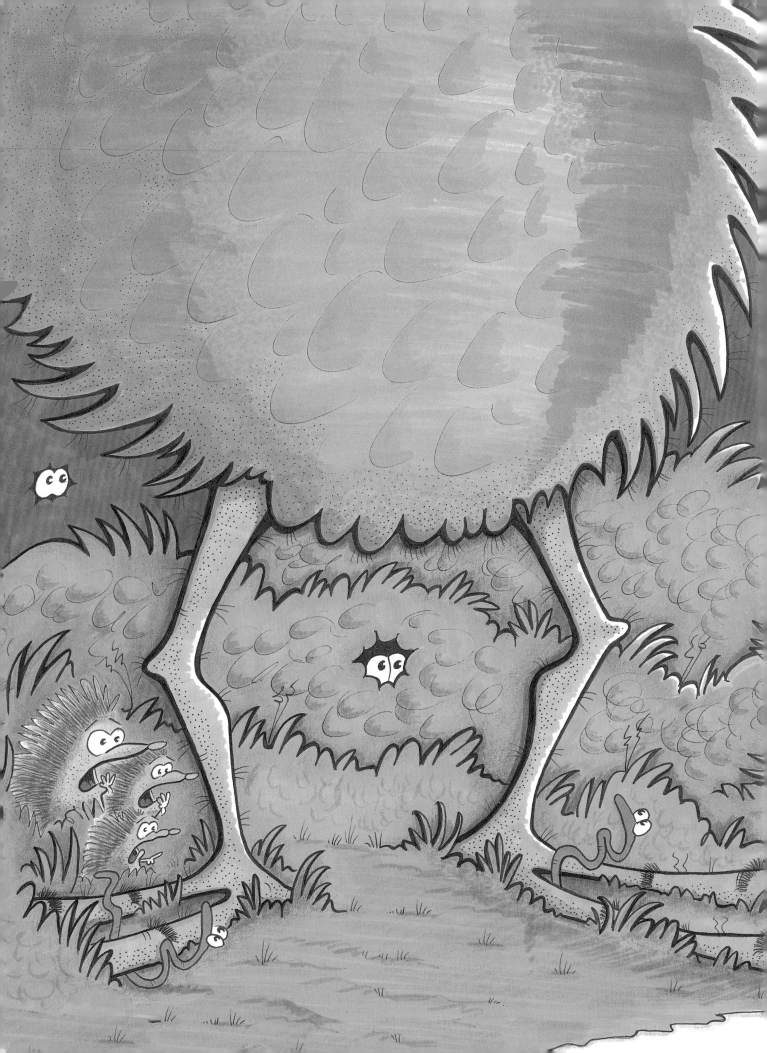

"**Who** are you?" Harry asked.

"I'm the Shmoogly Boo," said the monster.

"I'm not afraid of you," said Harry, and he held up both his fists.

The Shmoogly Boo burst into tears. "But I'm the Shmoogly Boo," he sobbed. "Everyone should be afraid of me, especially little boys."

Harry felt sorry for the monster. "Maybe if you had sharp teeth like a dinosaur, then I'd be afraid," he said.

So the Shmoogly Boo grew teeth that were big and long and as sharp as knives. He gnashed them together and shouted:

"BOO!"

"No, no, no," said Harry. "You're still not scary. Maybe if you had a yellow and black stripy coat and a nasty sting in your tail like a bee, that might do it."

So the Shmoogly Boo grew a coat with stripes and a nasty, big sting. He buzzed and he gnashed his teeth and shouted:

"BOO!"

Harry shook his head and said, "I'm still not afraid. Maybe if you had pointed ears like a hungry wolf that would scare me."

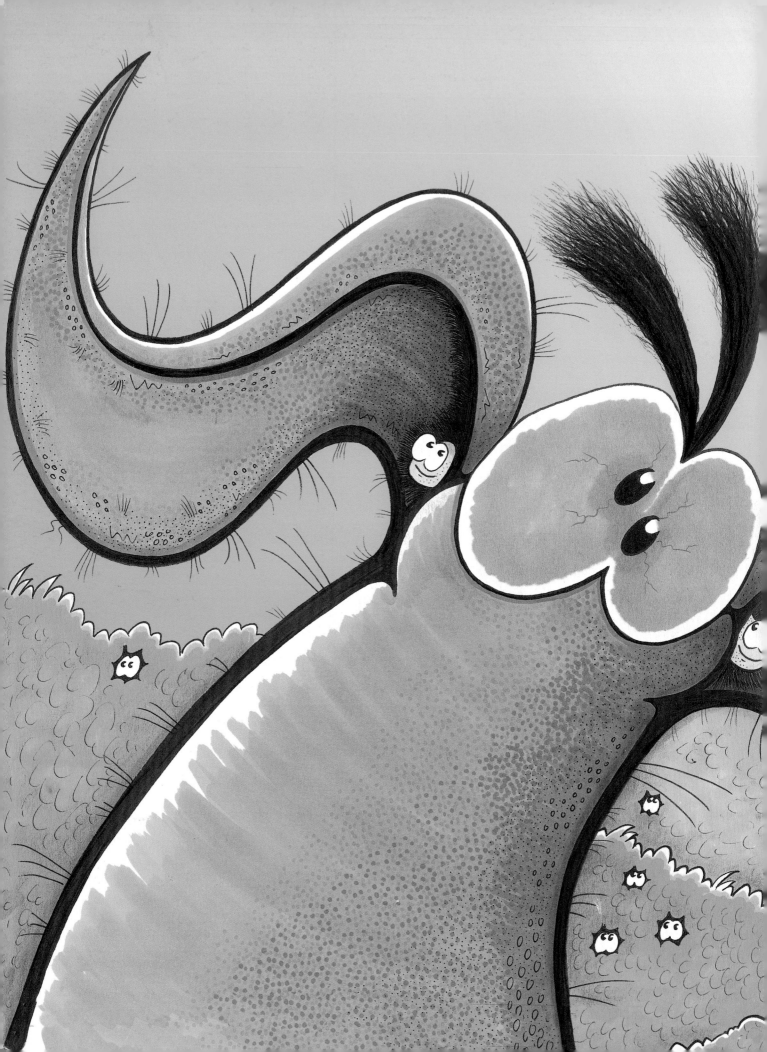

So the Shmoogly Boo grew pointed ears like a wolf. He buzzed and gnashed his teeth, and he waved his pointy ears and shouted:

"**BOO!**"

"I think it's the 'Boo'," said Harry. "Maybe if you had a loud roar like an angry lion, then I'd be really scared."

So the Shmoogly Boo grew
a long, golden mane and
practised roaring loudly. He
buzzed like a bee, gnashed his
sharp teeth, waved his pointy
ears and roared:

"BOOAR

RRRR!"

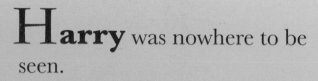

Harry was nowhere to be seen.

The Shmoogly Boo looked to his left; he looked to his right. He looked up, and he looked down. No little boy.

"HURRAY!"

"I scared him. I scared him with my loud, roaring lion voice, my pointy wolf ears, my stripy bee coat and my sharp dinosaur teeth," he cried.

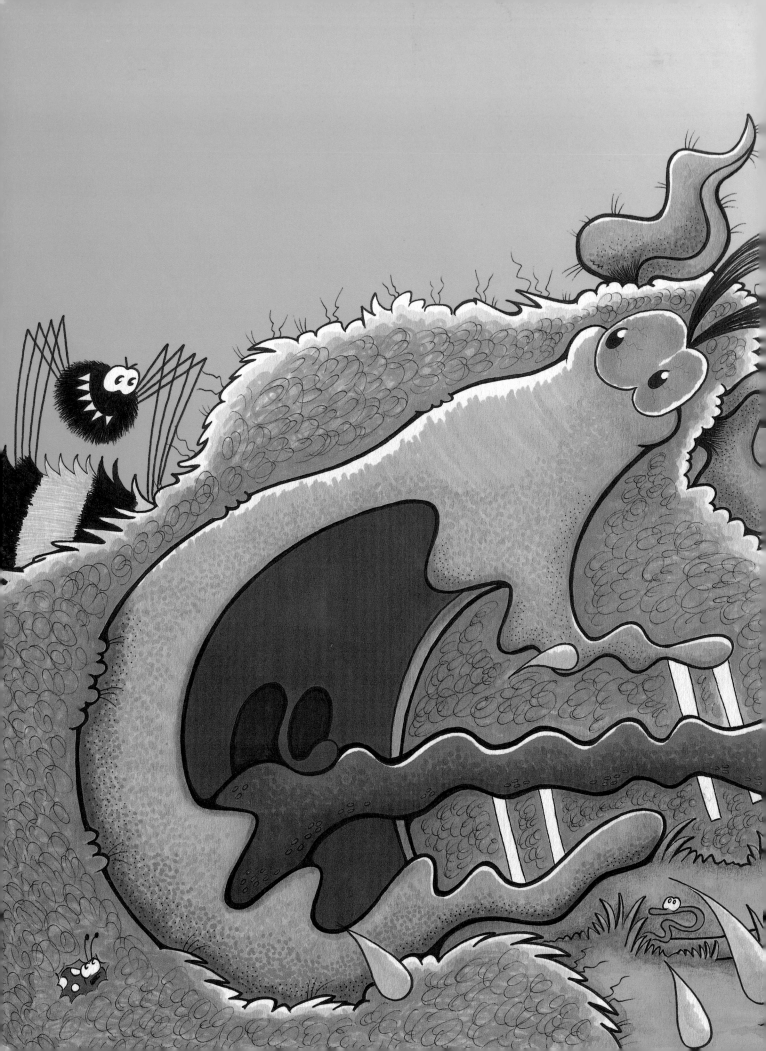

Then, from behind a tree, came a small, quivery voice: "L ... L ... Look behind you!"

The Shmoogly Boo looked. "I don't see anything," he said.

"There, on your back! A b ... big ... b ... b ... black ..."

For Roxanne, Leonni, Levi, Kaii and Eskiah - EW
For my son, Latham - DW

Published by
Hogs Back Books
The Stables
Down Place
Hogs Back
Guildford GU3 1DE
www.hogsbackbooks.com
Text copyright © 2016 Eileen Wharton
Illustrations copyright © 2016 David Walker
The moral right of Eileen Wharton to be identified as the author
and David Walker to be identified as the illustrator of this work has been asserted.
First published in Great Britain in 2016 by Hogs Back Books Ltd.
All rights reserved. No reproduction, copy or transmission
of this publication may be made without prior written permission.
No part of this publication may be reproduced, stored in a retrieval system,
or transmitted in any form or by any means, electronic, mechanical, photocopying,
recording or otherwise without the prior permission of the publisher.
Printed in Malta
ISBN: 978-1-907432-23-1
British Library Cataloguing-in-Publication Data.
A catalogue record for this book is available from the British Library.
1 3 5 4 2

**Further adventures
of the Shmoogly Boo coming soon**